DISNEY · PIXAR

Cars

Al's Sky-High Adventure

By Luke Paulson
Illustrated by Dave Boelke, Claudia di Genova, and Seung Kim
Designed by Tony Fejeran

Based on the characters and designs created by Pixar

Random House 🏠 New York

ISBN: 978-0-7364-2534-6

www.randomhouse.com/kids/disney

Printed in the United States of America
10 9 8 7 6 5 4 3 2 1

Al Oft, the Lightyear blimp, was hovering over the big stadium when he witnessed an amazing sight: superstar rookie Lightning McQueen was pushing a broken-down race car—The King himself!—across the finish line.

"Wow," thought Al. "That McQueen fella seems like a really nice car. Too bad he's leaving town."

Everyone at the racetrack knew who Al was.
The fans always cheered when he flew overhead.
But he was lonely up in the sky all by himself.

Al couldn't help admiring McQueen's pit crew. It was filled with the rookie's close friends. They had come all the way from Radiator Springs to support McQueen at his big race.

After the race season, Al decided to fly slowly over the countryside, looking at everything below and just enjoying the ride. Sometimes he even helped lost travelers. He had a good view from above and could guide the cars to their destinations.

One day, Al saw a little town below him that looked like the place McQueen had described. He flew low—and spotted McQueen himself!

"Hey, McQueen!" shouted a rusty old truck. "Lookee there! It's that Lightyear blimp from your big race!"

"Al, it's you! How are you doing, buddy? Welcome to Radiator Springs!" McQueen called up.

"My name's Mater. Like 'tuh-mater,' without the 'tuh'!" said the rusty truck. "Wanna help us round up a stray tractor that busted loose, Mr. Blimp?"

"Yeah," said McQueen. "We can't see where the lost tractor went. But I'll bet you can from up there!"

"Sure," said Al. "What does he look like?"

"A tractor that looks like he's lost," Mater replied.

Sure enough, from high in the sky, Al soon found the lost tractor. He lit up his sign to show McQueen that he had found him.

"Hey, that's great, Al, but we can't get over those big rocks!" McQueen shouted. "Can you see a way for us to get around them?"

Al looked down and all around. Sure enough, he soon found a path the two cars could take to reach the lost tractor. Within minutes, Mater and McQueen were guiding the tractor home.

"Now, this calls for a celebration, Al!" McQueen shouted. "We're having one of our neon cruises tonight. Why don't you join us?"

But Al just looked sadly at McQueen. "I can't cruise," he replied. "I'm too big and too high up."

"Sure you can!" said McQueen. "Just turn on your neon and fly low."

That night, Al turned on his sign and flew very low.

As the cars in Radiator Springs looked up at Al, McQueen introduced him. "That's my friend Al Oft, the Lightyear blimp. Just look at him. He's got the best neon you've ever seen."

"And you sure know how to cruise—low and slow!" Ramone told Al.

Al smiled. He was having the most fun he'd ever had. And with all his new friends, he knew he'd never be lonely again.